Okanagan Tall Tales

Written by Darcy Nybo

Illustrated by LeEtta LaFontaine

Team Published through
Artistic Warrior Publishing

For permission requests, email the publisher, with the subject "Attention: Permissions" at publisher@artisticwarrior.com

Ordering Information:
Special discounts are available on quantity purchases by corporations, associations, schools, and others. For details, contact the publisher at publisher@artisticwarrior.com

Single books can be purchased on Amazon.

Issued in print and electronic format.

ISBN 978-1-987982-02-2 (paperback)

ISBN 978-1-987982-09-1 (eBook)

Written by Darcy Nybo

Illustrated by LeEtta LaFontaine

First Edition

Created in Canada

AW
Okanagan Tall Tales is an Artistic Warrior Publication. Some stories in this book were included in Okanagan Tales in 2004, now out of print.

This book is dedicated to Nicole Nybo, my fellow Ogopogo spotter and favourite daughter.

Table of Contents

AUTHOR'S NOTE
The backstory on the stories

"Water Dragon"* took first place in an international short story contest back in 2003. It first appeared in *Tall Tales and Short Stories*, edited by Steven Van Bakel. This story was written because my daughter, then a young girl, asked me about the Ogopogo and how he got into Okanagan Lake. I couldn't find a good explanation, so I wrote the story.

"Remittance Man" was inspired by my curiosity as to who first settled in the Okanagan. While the story is fiction, the remittance men were a large part of the creation and growth of the towns and cities in the Okanagan. It was published as a series in the Westside Weekly newspaper back in 2010 and won a short story contest that same year.

"River Speaks"* was first published in June of 2004 in, *To Hope and Beyond*, published by the Penticton Writers and Publishers. It is part of a First Nations legend passed on to me by the kind people at Nk'Mip Desert and Heritage Centre in Osoyoos. I hope my version does the story justice.

"How Kalamalka Got Its Colours"* is a total gift of imagination. The lake is a beautiful sight and was named after a First Nations leader. Kal Tire, a tire franchise in Canada, was named after Kalamalka Lake.

"The Ghosts of Guisachan" is based on stories I heard from many locals about the sights and sounds they'd experienced when walking the tree-lined trail at Guisachan House. The history of this place is real, the ghosts . . . well you have to decide that for yourself.

"Naj and the Trickster" is another gift of imagination. The description of the hunting parties and the village is a reflection of how First Nations people lived in the Okanagan centuries ago.

"A Quail of a Tale"* is about as true a story as you will find in this collection. It has happened to many an Okanagan resident and it could happen to you. You have been warned.

*Published in Okanagan Tales in 2004. (Now out of print) Re-edited for Okanagan Tall Tales, 2019.

WATER DRAGON

Gather 'round dear reader and get cozy while I tell you the story of a gentle giant who lives in Okanagan Lake. Oh, I know, you've heard him compared to the Loch Ness Monster, but he's not like that at all. Truth is, neither is the one at Loch Ness, but that's another story for another time. Now get comfortable and kick your shoes off. That's it, nice and relaxed. Are you ready to start? Good.

It began a long, long time ago. Long before you or I or even our great, great, great grandparents were alive. It started so long ago that those who first told this story are now no more than dust. Did you know he had another name once? Oh yes, it's true. I believe it was in 1912 that someone first called him Ogopogo. Before that, the Salish people called him N'ha-a-itk or Naitaka. It means, sacred creature of water. When the others came to this land, they called him, Lake Demon. But I've strayed from the story I wanted to tell you.

Let me take you back, as far back as you can imagine going back. To the days before Majik and Glamour ruled. Back to when healers were simple folk. To the days before animals spoke and dragons flew. Did you know that dragons didn't always fly? Dragons were once creatures of the sea.

It began with one particular merdragon. His name was Mak'ata, and he was as fine a merdragon as anyone had ever seen. His neck was long and strong, his flippers sleek and swift. Mak'ata was also a dreamer. He dreamed of one day walking on land as the other great creatures did. He would watch them on the shore and dream of a life above water.

One morning he swam as close as he could to shore and flung himself onto the beach. The villagers heard a mighty crash that shook their huts to their foundation. What a sight it was. Can you imagine the uproar caused by finding a merdragon on your beach? The townsfolk rushed here and there, frantically trying to tie ropes about Mak'ata and drag him back to sea. The younger ones splashed buckets of water on him. Finally, one young lady, I believe her name was Lesas, ran for the town healer. Now remember, this was a very long time ago. The town healer was part doctor and part maker of Majik. It was quite common then for chants and spells to be cast just as often as potions were given to those in need of the healer's wisdom.

Healer arrived to find the townspeople heaving and puffing and muttering amongst themselves. All efforts to get the giant creature back to the sea had failed and they were growing tired. Healer knelt and stroked the creature's noble head. The creature looked forlorn and saddened by his failed attempt to gain the freedom the land creatures had. Healer gazed into his eyes and understood the soul of Mak'ata was pure, and his intentions were honourable. He shouted to the townspeople to bring blankets and soak them in water to lay upon the merdragon. The sun rose high in the sky and if they were to save him, they must move quickly. Healer sent Lesas back to his hut for more blankets, potions, and his Majik book. She ran swiftly and when she returned, helped the townspeople place the dampened blankets on Mak'ata. Healer motioned for her to come close and sit at his side. He lifted the great head of Mak'ata and laid it gently upon her lap.

Mak'ata could not keep his eyes off hers, nor she from his as Healer went about his work. Potions and oils were mixed, and chants were whispered as the sun blazed down upon them. Mak'ata felt his hide begin to dry and burn, yet he did not cry out. He lay there, content for the moment to stare into the eyes of his land angel, his Lesas.

Healer worked until sunset. He sat beside Mak'ata and placed his hand upon Mak'ata's mouth and bade him to speak. Mak'ata looked puzzled. He did not know how he understood Healer, but he knew these words as clearly as he knew the words of his own mother. He opened his parched lips and spoke for the first time. "Tapadh leat." Healer smiled and kissed the creature on his forehead. "You are quite welcome," he replied, and the townspeople cheered. Mak'ata had spoken to them in their ancient tongue and they were pleased.

Imagine the weariness of Mak'ata. A creature accustomed to floating in the sea, having lain in the sand an entire day. His skin was cracked and blistered, his head pounded, yet he was happy. He was safe with Healer and his land angel, Lesas. Healer ordered the blankets to be removed so he could take a closer look at the creature. Mak'ata lay still as Healer stroked his spine, massaged his fins, and applied oils to his mighty tail and body. The stars came out, yet Mak'ata saw only their reflections in Lesas's eyes. He lay helpless for hours with her eyes to hold him fast. He saw more in them than he had ever seen in another's eyes before. He saw her gentleness, her playfulness. He saw the tale of her family and her life. He saw her anger and her fears. He saw her love for nature and all creatures. He saw her soul. Most of all, he saw her love. From this bonding of vision was borne a love like no other had ever known before. A love of land creature and sea creature. And so it came to be that Mak'ata and Lesas fell in love.

The legend does not say how long they lay upon that beach. Some say it was days, other speak of weeks, and others say it was complete at the rising of the next sun. However it came to be, one day at the light of dawn, Mak'ata awoke from a restless sleep to find he had changed. His bottom fins had hardened and formed themselves into short, powerful legs. He stood, then tottered uneasily for a time, and then reached for Lesas. To his surprise he found his upper fins had changed into beautiful rainbow coloured wings. He caressed Lesas's soft face with his wing tip and then gathered her close to his heart.

And that is how one dragon came to be. They were not

fierce creatures born of fire and anger and hate. They were gentle and warm, born of love, passion and necessity.

From that day on, Mak'ata and Lesas were inseparable. He scooped her onto his back and they flew over villages and kingdoms, free from the stares of townspeople and wagging tongues of old men and women. At first their love was accepted, a great triumph over death they called it. As time passed and memories faded from the brilliance of that day, the doubts began to grow. Not natural was the most common phrase uttered. "Not natural," they'd say, every time the pair was spotted together. Not right for a creature such as Mak'ata to be with one of their own. Not natural at all. Not right.

Lesas heard their words and endured their curious stares. Her love for Mak'ata was pure and yet in her heart she knew it would not be enough. Their differences were too great. There was so much she wanted to share with him and could not.

Healer watched as her heart filled with sorrow and her love for Mak'ata was slowly pushed aside. He had a plan and called to her and bade her to come into his hut. She warmed herself by his fire as he explained what he could do for her. He mixed potions and scented oils and asked if she were certain of her love for Mak'ata. She was. Despite the risks, she could not bear to have her heart filled with sorrow. She was stranded between two worlds. There was no other choice.

Healer instructed her to lie on the skins in front of the fire and remove her clothing. Lesas did as she was told. She shivered despite the warmth. Healer fed her potions, some bitter and some sweet, which she readily took. He rubbed scented oils into her skin and wrapped her tightly in the same blanket she had once wrapped around Mak'ata. She fell into a gentle sleep and when she awoke at dawn, her skin was afire, and her head felt as if it would explode into a million shards of glass. She moaned and reached for Healer only to find she was outside. The sun shone down upon her from between the tall treetops. Shadows and light played across her vision as she tried to right herself. Unsteady, she stood and placed her arms out for balance. To her shock and delight she found beautiful rainbow wings instead of arms. Her soft silky skin was now coarse and scaly. Her long shapely legs now squat and strong. Her beautiful fingers and toes were now claws. She tilted her head and cried out to the morning light. "Mak'ata!"

That is how the Majik of the dragons came to be. Mak'ata and Lesas lived a very, very, very long time. They had many children and their children had children, and so the lineage progressed until the time when Majik and Glamour reached their peak.

This was the time of great magicians. The years had turned Healers into great and powerful witches, sorcerers, and wizards. Vast kingdoms had sprung up throughout the land and kings, knights, and maidens took advantage of these sumptuous times. Dragons were plentiful and they spoke in the native tongue of the lands they inhabited. Woodland creatures gained the power of speech, but would only speak to those pure of heart.

As I said before, it was a time of great Majik. But sadly, the time of great magicians was fraught with barbarian acts. People did not appreciate the Majik. It had become commonplace.

Instead of becoming one with all things in nature, they became ignorant and frivolous. It was a time when young men proved their virility and honour by slaying something larger and greater than themselves. Unfortunately, that meant the dragons' lives were now in danger.

The offspring of Mak'ata and Lesas went into hiding. When children were born, they were kept deep in caves or high upon mountains until their flying skills were such that they could escape the thrusted lance of an honour-seeking knight. Despite the blood lust around them, it was a happy time for most. Food was plentiful, the earth was warm, and life was everywhere.

It was at this time when the great, great, great, great grandson of Mak'ata and Lesas began to search for his truth. His name was Lotad'h. He was brave and swift in flight. He could snatch a deer from the meadow and mercifully kill it before it knew it was dinner. His touch was gentle enough to save a fallen sparrow chick from the nest and put it safely back with its kin.

Lotad'h was very fast and because of this he became the dragon to hunt. Anyone who could hunt and kill Lotad'h would be proclaimed the bravest, fastest, and most honourable of all knights in the land. So, it came to be that one creature's greatest attributes also became his greatest failing. His family begged him to hide. Go to the mountains they said, or down to the sea. Lotad'h considered their warnings. Perhaps it would be best if he did leave for a time. After all, dragons live for hundreds, perhaps thousands of years. Surely, they would forget about him once this human generation had passed into dust.

And so it was that Lotad'h started on his journey that eventually brought him here to us.

He flew by night and slept in caves by day. Near daybreak of the fourth day he found himself near a castle in a great land. Not wanting to be seen, he secreted himself in a small cave on the mountainside. As he drifted off to sleep, he heard a sound outside the cave. He warily inched forward to find a young maiden sitting nearby. She sat to the right of him, seemingly unaware of his presence.

Lotad'h sniffed. A glorious smell wafted from this human creature. A smell like he had never encountered before. He darted his tongue out in order to taste the odour of this new, magnificent thing. The sweetness of it filled his head and caused him to sigh the happiest of sighs. Still the maiden did not move. Lotad'h crept closer until he could see the object that emanated the delicious aroma. The maiden was eating something round. It was red in some parts, orange in others, and again yellow in others. The flesh inside was a creamy orange . . . and that smell. Oh, that astounding, phenomenal smell! Lotad'h sniffed again, inching closer to the maiden. He was no longer afraid. He did not care if he frightened her or if he was found, his only thought was to be near the succulent perfume that wafted up from this precious food.

He flicked his tongue towards the fruit. As he did so, the maiden turned to him and smiled. She showed no fear, no sign that she had been caught off guard. Lotad'h jerked his head back so quickly that it bounced off the roof of the cave and then hit grass with a thud. He shook his head and gave his best dragon smile to the lady.

She smiled back and showed him another lush orb. Lotad'h could not believe what was being offered. His mouth watered and his tongue lolled out of his mouth. Perhaps a small taste wouldn't hurt. He inched forward until his head was near the maiden's shoulder. He sighed as she turned and offered the prize to him. Gently, he took the fruit into his mouth, his tongue caressing its velvet outer coating. Oh, what joy! What an utter and complete wonder this food. It must be from the gods for only gods could create such a thing. He gently bit into the flesh. The juice gushed into every corner of his mouth, flooding his senses with sweetness he'd never known before.

It is said that Lotad'h actually moaned with pleasure as he ate. Once he had consumed every drop of juice, every fibre of flesh, he turned to the maiden and thanked her. She gestured to him with her hands that he was welcome. Lotad'h spoke again and asked for her name. Again, she made quick gestures with her hands but spoke not. Lotad'h understood. She could not speak.

"I shall give you a name then," he proclaimed. "I shall call you Surkshati and you shall be my friend." Surkshati clapped her hands together in what Lotad'h assumed to be acceptance. Within seconds Lotad'h was surrounded by lances, spears, and flaming torches. It was a trap and Lotad'h was caught. They tied him firmly and led him to a large cage inside the castle stadium. He was to fight the brave and bold knights of the kingdom. Winner to take the hand of the fair maiden who had baited their trap. Lotad'h was humbled. He was ashamed for his weakness and yet somehow still longed for just one more taste of the velvet coated fruit.

Later that day, Lotad'h heard the chant of the crowds. He was led into a large bowl-shaped arena. A knight entered opposite him. The crowd cheered even louder. Lotad'h raised himself up to his highest height and ran at the knight. The knight thrust his sword, missed, and turned to face Lotad'h again. Lotad'h was not there. He had broken his bonds, taken flight and was winging his way up and out of the arena. He flew as fast as he could, away from his family, his homeland, and all he loved. He flew away from the boorish knights, away from the Glamour and the Majik. Away from it all.

He travelled many days and nights and found himself in the land of his ancestor Mak'ata. He landed on the beach where Mak'ata was first found and prayed to his ancestor. He wanted to forget about being a dragon. He wanted to hide forever. He wanted to go back to the sea. "Take me back!" he cried. "We do not belong out here. The world has lost its gentle ways."

He waited for days but no one answered. Lotad'h was alone. Without direction or purpose, he took to the sky over the sea. He flew non-stop, day and night. If he hungered, he did not eat. If he tired, he did not show it. For many miles all he saw below him was ocean. Nothing but the dark rolling sea which would not take him back. Some days later there was land, a land whose look was unfamiliar. A land he had no wish to be a part of. On he flew until one day he could fly no more and he plummeted towards the earth. His heart was tired, and he was grateful for death.

Instead of hitting the earth, Lotad'h found himself falling through water. He felt himself changing as claws and legs turned to fins. His scales filled with the fresh lake water and began to smooth out over his frame. His eyes sparkled as he realized what had happened. His ancestors had heard his plea. He was home.

And that, dear reader, is how the Okanagan Ogopogo came to be. You don't have to believe this story. Many don't, but the ones who do believe have seen him. They know he exists.

If you look closely at the reports of his sighting, he appears most often around Peachland. In late summer, down on the docks, you'll find the ones who believe. Late at night they toss their freshly picked peaches into the lake – a treat for Ogopogo.

REMMITANCE MAN

The name's Frank. Not Francis or François, no, not one of those. Funny, I can remember my Christian name, but not my family name. It's just as well, my family was happy to be rid of me. I was a bit of a scoundrel according to my sainted mother who felt that drink was the devil's own tool. Add to that, two older brothers, and me not giving a lick about the shipping business, and my fate was sealed.

My father owned the largest shipping company in Bristol. The temperamental ocean, the salty air, playing polo and fox hunts; these were the things of my youth. It's a wonder I survived the dry scruffy land of the Canadian Okanagan. It was, despite my complaining, my own fault. I didn't really care for my father's business. I saw it as a way to support me, even after I became a man. Collecting numbers and writing them in a book was nothing compared to gathering words and turning them into stories. I would wander the seaside, composing in my head, and sometimes even on paper, until it was dusk. Then my mates and I would wander down to the pub. It was a good life, back then.

That way of life was cut short in 1910, when my mother picked up the Bristol Courier. Right there, in black and white, for all the world to see, was the story of two young men who had gone on a spree of sorts. They were drinking and cavorting and causing such a ruckus that at the end of the night two pubs had banned them and three fellows, including myself, had ended up at the local hospital. It was a grand night and I had the broken nose to prove it.

The Ladies Garden Club was meeting in the parlour when I arrived home. It was foolish of me to just walk right in. Mother took one look at me, ripped trousers and plaster across my nose, and that was it. She ushered me out and asked my oldest brother, Thomas, to escort me to my rooms. There were hushed tones and whispers from the ladies in the parlour and I could feel the righteous biddies gossiping about me and how I'd shamed my family name. It wasn't my fault they didn't know how to enjoy life! Joseph, barely two years my elder, was assigned to watch me after that. Thomas was busy at father's offices.

It was easy to lose Joseph. He tired easily and believed me every time I went to my rooms. I'd slip down the back stairs and leave through the servant's entrance and off to the pubs I'd go.

I kept my nose clean and my fists in my pockets after that, and if it weren't for a newly acquired love for gambling, my nights out with the lads would have remained a secret. But alas, it was not to be. Apparently, the Reverend Johnston's son had a tug at his conscience and told his father that he'd taken money from the church to play cards with me and the lads. They say confession is good for the soul, but it wasn't good for my soul.

The Reverend told my father and the rest was history. It wasn't like I was of value to the family in any way. I was the scoundrel, the laggard, the black sheep. Thomas was newly married, knickers deep in father's business and on top of it all, he was about to become a first-time father. With my luck it would be a son. Joseph was seeing some young woman from the next county and we all knew he'd be next. Me, well the only time a woman lasted more than a night with me is when I fell asleep in her rooms and I awoke beside her in the morning.

I tried to soften Mother up and explain that the drink had gotten the best of me and it would never happen again. Funny how I remember my last days in Bristol, but not my family name. Just as well as it would cause my brother's children's, children's children shame in the telling. Then again, these are more lenient times.

Mother couldn't be swayed, and Father was so angry he would not speak to me. He had a shipment headed to Canada in a week's time. I was to be on that ship, a healthy allowance in my pocket. I was to receive this allowance every week on the grounds that I not return home until I'd mended my ways and made good of myself.

I was to cross this new land and find my way in a place called the Okanagan. They told me it was a land of lakes and sunshine and pioneer spirit. I could start a new life there, away from my reputation and make my family proud. Although I wasn't too keen on leaving my home, my rooms, my mates, I was excited by the prospect of adventure. After all, how hard could it be?

The trip in and of itself was rather uneventful. I spent the first three days in my bunk trying not to churn out what little food I could take in. My bunk mate, James, told me there were some high stakes card games and some mighty fine drink to be had once I had my sea legs. Three days later I joined in and spent the rest of my journey with the grandest group of lads you'll ever find. We were all going to start a new life. What a motley crew we were. We joked that Australia was founded by thieves and murderers and Canada would be founded by rogues and drunkards.

The cards were good to me and when we arrived in Halifax my pockets were a bit richer than when I'd left. My shipmates and I swaggered through town, hit the pubs, sweet talked the ladies and finally, after a night which cost me a fair bit of coin, I boarded a train headed west. For the most part the trip was uneventful, plenty of drink and cards to keep a young man busy. At some stops ladies would board the train and entertain us, always leaving us with a little less money than we'd started with.

By the time we'd reached Calgary I was skint. I sent word

home and within two days my pockets were full again. The journey to the Okanagan was much the same as the trip to Calgary, save with a few more mountains and lakes and less women to keep us company.

Finally, we arrived in Peachland, just in time to witness the building of the eight-sided Baptist church. It was a fine sight to see, from the outside anyway. I never did set foot inside, as I belonged to the Church of England. Not that I attended church at home, but it was what I told the local nosey parkers when they asked.

James and I became thick as thieves and bought land next to each other. Mine was too hilly and sandy to be any good, but what did I care; I wasn't going to do much with it anyway. My nearest neighbours were Walter and Elyse. He was from England, she from Germany. Their lives would tear apart in four years, but for now they were happy. Walter didn't drink or gamble or even smoke, but I liked his company just the same. He was a good one for information. It was through him that I got my cabin built and was able to purchase a few good riding horses and some old hounds from a recently deceased lad from Cardiff. It appears his liver wasn't as game for drink as he was.

I planted a few trees, with Walter's help, and wrote home to the family to let them know I was an orchardist now, doing an honest day's work, or at least Walter was. It was a beautiful setup over the next few years. I would tell them of the apple and cherry and peach trees and how I needed more money for tilling equipment and ladders and buckets and such. Young orchards took time to grow and I was more than happy to hand the tending of them over to Walter for a weekly stipend. He worked for far less than I would, and when he found Elyse was with child he garnered as much work as possible from me. This suited me just fine as my time was better spent at the pub and riding with my fellow remittance men.

Did I mentionr emittance men was what they called us, because we lived off our families money. It was never said with kindness. When it flew from their mouths it was usually uttered in distaste by the local farmers who said it out of jealousy as they worked hard for little money. It was also whispered behind gloved hands by the young church ladies who secretly wanted to return to our cabins with us to experience the desires of the flesh. At least that's what we told ourselves. We never could convince them to come.

For the most part I was able to get along well with the town folk. I had a prim accent, was well cultured, educated, and came from an upper-middle-class background. I got involved with the local theatre group and directed a few plays and bedded a few leading ladies, though not the ones from the new church. It was all very hush, hush of course.

Mostly, I had a carefree life. Walter did the hard work on the land and I spent my days hunting and fishing, and my nights at the pubs or dancing at the town balls. As soon as Elyse gave birth to one child, she'd be bloated with another and in the time I knew them she gave birth to two boys and a girl, and one that was so badly deformed they didn't know what it was. Walter buried it on the property line between our places. James said he couldn't have it near his as it turned him into a willie-boy just thinking about it. James and I soon forgot about it and come winter we spent most of our time in the pubs and provided entertainment for the town gossips.

That all changed in the autumn of 1914. There was a fellow in town with a ham radio and he gave us the news that Britain and the Commonwealth had declared war on Imperial Germany. Walter and Elyse could be heard clear to the bottom of the hill and into the town as they argued. He wanted to go help fight for his country, to kill people from her country. They weren't the only ones. There were plenty of couples in the area where English married German and vice versa.

Now even though we shunned work, we remittance men now had a chance to redeem ourselves. As enjoyable as fishing and drinking in the summer and dancing and drinking in the winter was, we missed our home and our old lives.

One of the lads, I'm pretty sure it was James (we'd been heavily into the drink that night), came up with a plan. We formed a pact, the pact of the remittance men. Word spread fast and soon hundreds of us from across the valley were ready. It was a grand plan and it would work. It was our duty to protect our homeland. We'd either die heroes or return to our homes alive and redeemed in the eyes of our families.

The plan was simple. We withdrew all of our savings from the local banks and placed most of the money in mason jars. We buried them in exactly the same spot on each of our plots of land. Eight paces west and seventeen paces north of our cabin doors. All traces of our lives there were to be wiped out. However, none of us could imagine destroying that which was our own. We agreed that we would do it for each other. The next day we rose, mounted our best horses, grabbed our rifles, and headed to the nearest remittance man's cabin. Once there, we dismounted and killed the hunting dogs and horses as the valley residents would have no use for them. We simply couldn't bear to do it to our own.

Shots rang out across the valley at precisely eight o'clock in the morning. Then each remittance man poured kerosene across their neighbour's floorboards and set the cabin on fire. I can still recall the look of the boards as the oil soaked into them, thirsty for any type of moisture. I remember the whoosh as I dropped the match. The cabins burned to the ground in no time at all. All that was left was the faint smell of burned kerosene and outlines of feather mattresses. By 8:30 that morning, each and every remittance man had torched another remittance man's cabin and killed his animals. We rendezvoused down at the train station to catch the 9:15 going home. We gave our mounts to whoever was nearby. I remember I gave mine to a boy, no older than seven or eight. I'll never forget the look on his face when I told him the horse was his to keep.

All of this, this plan, was a symbol to us and to the people who looked down at us. We were walking away from our wild ways, destroying our past, and heading to a better future.

Then we rode the train to war.

Oh, the camaraderie we felt. It was heady. We were going to fight for our country, to prove ourselves, we were going home. Ah, but I can sense I've left you wondering about the money we buried. Well, we had to have a backup plan as no single plan is foolproof. James suggested that should we be lucky enough to live through the war and unlucky enough to not be welcomed back into the bosom of our families, we would return here, dig up the money and head out to the west coast where the weather was less barbaric and the lifestyle more to our liking. After all, no one knew what the war would bring. Our families might not be there to send us money when the war ended.

So off we went. The return trip took only two weeks. I never saw battle. On the way back I became ill and by the time we reached port in my beloved England, I was weak with the fever. I arrived at my family home and was set up in my old rooms. My brother, Thomas, now a father of two rambunctious boys, was pardoned from going off to war in order to work for the King's navy out of father's offices. Joseph, my compliant middle brother returned home with half his leg and half his brain blown away. I remember my mother wandering the halls, asking God why this had happened to her. The daft woman never did realize that it was us who were half dead, not her.

Joseph had a hard time recognizing he was back at home. When I was with fever, I thought his ramblings were simply in my own head. As my fever lessened, I realized my brother had gone quite mad.

I remember that last night. The doctor informed my mother that I was on the mend. I wouldn't be able to go off to war, but I would live, we all would, so long as the Germans were poor shots and missed our home with their bombs. Mother didn't find his humour amusing at all.

Once the doctor left, Mother retired to her rooms and the

house was quiet. I heard Joseph thumping down the hallway on his crutches as he normally did at that time of night. He came into my rooms and then to my bedside. He sat down beside me and muttered something about taking cover. Then he turned to me and smiled. "I know who you are." He said it with a quiet certainty that chilled me to the core. "You're one of those Imperial Germans in disguise." I have a faint recollection of him leaning over me with a smug look on his face.

There was a loud noise and a flash, or was it a flash and a loud noise, it's hard to recall now. The next thing I knew I was here, standing on this hillside in front of my burned cabin. I looked around and saw the rotting carcasses of my hounds and my old horse. I thought about Walter and was immediately standing in his kitchen. There stood Elyse, children playing at her feet, cooking up a noxious smelling broth. Walter was gone.

I've been here ever since, wandering the hills and valleys of the Okanagan. The hills have changed over the years. Much has changed. Right here, where my cabin was, is a vineyard. They grow grapes and turn them into wine. Just my luck I can't drink a drop of it.

Over there, something they call a single-family housing development, is on James's land. I'm not sure if that means the head of the family is single or if it's because the houses aren't joined, but there are lots of people there, and dogs, and cats, and children. I never did find out what happened to James, or to Walter. I often wonder if Walter ever got to war and if he ever killed any of Elyse's kin. As I recall, Elyse moved away with a nice man from town, a German fellow. He took her kids, too, which was very decent of him.

Every now and then, especially on crisp autumn nights, I think I hear James's voice telling me to come play cards, or Walter telling me he's come back for Elyse, but they are merely whispers of a mind slowly sinking into madness. It's been over one-hundred years now. That's far too long to wander without even knowing my last name. I want to leave this place, but I don't know how. Can you help me find my way back home?

My name is Okanagan. I am a river. I am here to tell you a story about the way things came to be in a place now called, Okanagan Falls.

A long, long time ago I was a grand, flowing river. There was a time when I flowed freely and became one with others until we joined with the sea. We travelled over two countries, we knew no borders, and we rejoiced in the becoming of the one. We still join, we still make our journey, but it is not the same.

My story starts in a time when the people were new to this land and many powerful creatures roamed freely. Despite the multitude of different beasts, we lived in harmony together. The valley was peaceful then. Animals came to me in great numbers. They drank from me, taught their young on my banks, and grew old and died by my side. The people respected me and sometimes they feared me.

We were happy then: Wind, Sun, Land, Sky and me. One day a whisper of news came with Wind. There was a tale of a great creature. His name was Coyote or Senk'lip and he was to bring the king of all fish to my river. This was news that could benefit all who lived and played by my banks and I told Wind to spread the word across the land. The people heard, but they did not understand.

Sun bore down upon me and my water was given up in thanks for the warmth it gave my shores. Days later Sky gave it back again and the land grew lush and green.

With each new rain, new tales fell upon me. Tales of a shape changer who tricked women and coaxed his king fish to come up the streams and rivers of our valley. He was cunning and swift and anxious to find a wife.

I felt other stories, too. There were stories of happiness

and sorrow, forgiveness and anger, battles won and babies born. I tasted the salt of the sea and the fruit of exotic lands. I gained all this from the rains. Still, the one story that came loudest of all was the story of Senk'lip.

He was nearer now. The king of fish were coming and Senk'lip named them salmon. They would feed the animals and people of my banks. The animals gathered and drank this knowledge from me and waited for the great Senk'lip and the salmon he would bring. The people sensed a change, but did not know what to do, so they did nothing.

With each passing day the tales became fiercer and angrier. Senk'lip wanted a bride. He approached the leaders of many a village and asked for one of their daughters to be his wife. At every village he was denied. Not one wished to be joined for life to a temperamental shape shifter, and their parents honoured their daughters' decisions. This made Senk'lip very angry and his anger poured from him in vicious retributions. Senk'lip punished the villages by blocking their streams with great stone barriers so that no salmon would ever reach their shores.

Tales of his anger eclipsed the fact that the king of fish were coming with him. I tried not to listen to the tales of anger. I wanted only to hear of the salmon. Time after time the tales came, each one more fantastic than the last. We could not believe his anger was so strong.

"He is lonely," whispered Wind.

"He is young," gleamed Sun.

"He is dangerous," said the Land.

"He is almost here," said the Sky.

I told them all, "We must warn those who dwell here. His anger shall arrive before him and we must be prepared."

Wind was the first to try. She whipped around the villagers and pushed them away from me, but they would not leave. Sun tried next and shone so bright that his reflection off my waters blinded them, and still they did not leave. Land shook violently, toppling trees and causing great cracks in the stones. The people left for a time, and then came back because it was their home. Then Wind and I thrashed wildly together creating a terrible storm. Sky joined with us and large, heavy clouds moved in. Thunder and Lightning completed the barrage and still, the people would not leave.

"We have done all we can," said Sun. "Now we must wait and see how great this Coyote fares against the will of these brave people."

The next day I felt Senk'lip enter me from downstream. I waited. His anger was like a bitter root thrown into a pot of winter potatoes. I felt foul and tried to drown him. I rose up against him, pulling him under, trying to keep him away from my people. I was no match for his powers and he escaped without harm. The king fish were with him.

Clouds moved in to block the sun and chill the air, but the people came to my banks to conduct their daily business. We watched with anticipation as Senk'lip left my waters and rose up on the bank and walked among them.

"I am Senk'lip and I bring with me the king of all fish. With these fish in your river you will never go hungry. Let me join you at your fires." Senk'lip reached into the river with his great hands and scooped out two large salmon.

The villagers brought him to their fires and he showed them how to cook the salmon. He instructed that the salmon must be roasted on a spit and slowly turned over open flames. To be given up this way made the salmon proud to offer its life for the people.

The women brought roots, berries and greens to the fire and all was put together in a feast to celebrate the coming of the king of fish and the arrival of the great Coyote. The children ran and danced, the men offered up the pipe and the women sang songs.

Soon it was nightfall and time for the people to sleep. The leader of the people offered Senk'lip his tent. Senk'lip denied his offer and spoke to the entire village.

"I do not require a place to sleep. I do not ask for your refuge. I offer your village great foods and all I ask in return is one of your daughters as my wife." Senk'lip pointed to a group of young women gathered around an older man.

"These will do. Who are the fathers of these young women? I would have one of them as my bride. It is little to ask in return for the king fish."

The young women looked up at Senk'lip, giggled, then ran off to sit at their respective mothers' sides. After many agonizing moments, one of the fathers stood and walked over to Senk'lip.

"We have little food and we must work hard for it. Our daughters are worth more to us than easy work and a full belly. You ask us to sell one of our children for fish. Leave us!"

Senk'lip was furious. He roared at the father. The father stood his ground. Senk'lip turned and rushed towards my banks.

"You will never again eat my salmon!" He howled at the villagers and dove into my depths. The moonlight shone upon the waters so that all could see. The surface boiled and churned. A formidable sound bubbled up from my depths and then exploded as tons of rocks were forced upwards. Water overflowed the banks and the people were afraid.

Senk'lip bounded out of the water and stood atop the rocks he had recently placed there. Water glistened off his hair and skin. His face was snarled in anger. "NEVER!" He screamed and dove back into my water.

My river bottom shifted, the rock shores collapsed into him, and yet he survived. He was moving me, altering me into something I was not. I thought of my people, my animals, my friends and I rushed around him. I tried with all my might to hold him down to stop the transformation.

A horrible grinding sound filled me as more rock was pushed upwards beside the first barrier. My grasp on him weakened as a part of me was remade into a raging waterfall. I gazed up and saw Senk'lip climb to the top of the peak, shake himself off, and stride away from the village.

His anger changed me forever and the Okanagan Falls were born.

The rest of my story is not as spectacular. You will find that most of life is that way, too. Over the years Wind and I worked together to wear down the rocks until the falls were smaller and allowed the salmon to spawn. They were a beautiful sight to see. The people rejoiced and ate well and Senk'lip faded into history as a legend. I never saw him again but there was a whisper brought on Wind that a young woman had agreed to be his bride. I like to think he finally found happiness.

My banks still nurture the animals and people of this valley, but it is different now. Many years passed and more people came and made their home close to my shore. Each year Sun would melt snow, Wind would blow the clouds into the valley, and Sky would release the rain. Then I would flow over the Land with the joy of the coming spring.

The new people didn't like our celebration. They called it a flood and blasted my beautiful falls away.

Wind said it was because the people wanted to live closer to me.

Sun said it was because they remembered how it used to be.

Land said that all things change.

Sky said they should learn to swim.

HOW KALAMALKA GOT ITS COLOURS

The Okanagan has many beautiful lakes, but none more beautiful than Kalamalka Lake, located between Vernon and Kelowna, off Highway 97.

If you ask how it got its colours people will likely tell you the scientific story. They'll tell you the lake is known as a, marl lake. When the lake warms in the summer, dissolved limestone forms crystals that reflect the sunlight. This is what creates its distinct blue-green colour. It's a nice scientific explanation, but I have a different story.

Many, many years ago, long before cars and highways and even tourists, there were only First Nations people living in this beautiful valley. Most were nomadic. They foraged and hunted the entire valley from north to south. A few stayed in one spot and harvested the land.

There was one small village on the west side of Kalamalka Lake. In this village was a beautiful young woman named, Unee. She lived in a kekuli, which is a home built into the earth and the side of hills.

She was a good daughter and older sister. She worked hard in the home and in the fields. It was said she would someday marry the son of the village leader.

Unee had no thoughts of marriage. She was happy in her own family. She loved the forest and in her spare time, would sit quietly on a rock in the sun, waiting to catch a glimpse of the many creatures that lived nearby. The animals came to trust her and by the time she was fifteen, she was able to sit amongst them without either having fear of the other. Her brother began to call her Tall Fox, for when she sat in the sun, her hair reflected a deep and warm crimson that matched a small red fox who would come to sit beside her.

One day the travelling people came to stay at the village. They were a hearty and robust bunch. The men laughed loudly and the women dressed brightly. They brought newness to the little village by the lake.

The leaders welcomed them and a great celebration was planned. Unee's parents were very excited. The travellers had brought squaw currant berries from the south and were happy to exchange them for poultices made from the arrowleaf balsamroot. Unee's mother, M'hati, was somewhat of a legend and made the best medicines in the valley. She was also very creative when it came to making delicious treats with the sweet berries the travellers were offering.

That night, Unee sat at the edge of the celebration, smiling as children ran and played and the elders traded goods and stories. She jumped when a young man touched her lightly on the shoulder.

He smiled and bowed his head before her. "Please excuse my presence, I did not mean to frighten you. I had to touch you to see if you were real. I have been watching you and I thought you were a forest spirit. I had to find out. I hope you understand. My name is Nven and I ask your forgiveness."

After a moment Unee spoke. "You did not frighten me. I was only a little startled. I was watching and when I watch I don't hear well. My name is Unee and you are forgiven."

The young man sat down beside her. "If I were to stop listening when I was looking, I would not be alive to startle you."

Unee stared at him. "Why would you not be alive. Who would want to kill you?"

"If I did not hear a bear or cougar come up from behind while I was hunting the deer, I would surely be dead by now. The hunter becomes the hunted if they don't pay attention."

Unee nodded and looked towards the celebration. "I have never hunted. I do not know of these things. I do not think I will ever hunt. The roots and berries are abundant here and we have more than enough fish. Our lake is filled with salmon and trout."

The fires died down and the singing and dancing stopped. It was time to rest for the night. Nven stood and looked down at Unee. "You are more beautiful up close than from afar. I cannot believe my luck at finding you." Nven stroked her long, black hair as his eyes explored and memorized her face. "There is word that traders are coming this way. They are different than us. Be careful of them." Nven took her by the hands and brought her to stand with him. "I must go." He bowed his head, released her hands and walked away. Unee watched him go and felt an odd stirring in her heart.

The next day Unee sat on her favourite rock and waited for the animals to come. A young mink approached her from the east and the small red fox from the west. This time she listened as she watched and soon she heard someone approaching from the north. Mink and fox retreated to the edge of the forest as Nven entered the clearing.

Unee smiled as he came and sat beside her. "We are leaving tomorrow," he said, head bowed. "There is something I must ask of you."

Unee lifted his chin so their eyes could meet. "Why do you not look at me? Even the fox meets my eyes when we are together."

"You are more beautiful by day than you are by night and I cannot look at you for every time I do, I am blinded by your beauty. I do not say this for your pleasure. It is my truth. From the moment I saw you, I wanted you for my wife." He held her gaze and swallowed. "Unee, come with me, travel with us. Be my wife."

Unee's heart pounded in her chest, her eyes fixed on Nven. "I hardly know you and yet I believe you speak your truth. I need time to think. I have never wanted to be a wife and now you come to our village and ask me to do what I have never dreamed. You ask me to be wife and nomad when all I wish is to stay and sit alone with the animals of the forest."

Nven nodded. "The days are getting colder and I must return to the south. Think of me. Think of a life with me. I will return for you in the spring and will send my love and devotion to you on the winds." He stood and touched her hair, then turned and walked back into the woods.

Unee did not know what to think. This young man was handsome and strong, and she did feel a stirring within, but what did it mean? She went to M'hati and asked for advice. Her mother's words were carefully chosen.

"Unee, some things come to us without our asking. Your young man has a patience as great as yours. For as you sat and waited for the animals to accept you, so he waits for you to accept him. You may not have been looking for a husband, but he has found you and now you must decide. Whatever your choice, make it wisely." Her mother hugged her close and kissed her cheeks. "Now go find your brother and tell him it is time to eat."

Unee spent the entire evening with Nven. They talked and laughed as the moon rose high in the sky. She was growing fond of him and if she allowed herself, she could imagine a life with him. They spoke of their childhoods and their dreams. Nven learned that Unee could to speak with the animals. Unee learned that Nven was becoming an expert horseman. The moon began to set and it was time for sleep. Tomorrow Nven and his family would begin their long journey south.

Nven kissed her gently on the cheek as they parted for the evening. "I will be back for you, Unee, and when I come, I know you will say yes."

"When you come back, I shall teach you to listen to the animals and they will tell you my answer." Unee kissed him quickly on the mouth and ran to her home.

Winter came quietly. The snow blanketed the forest, the animals settled in for the season, and Unee began to dream of a new life with Nven. Time passed and soon the earth turned towards the sun once more, bring warmer, longer days.

Unee continued to speak with the animals. One day in early spring, the little red fox came out of her burrow and sat at her feet. Unee told her she was in love and had decided to marry Nven. Unee listened as fox told her of a litter of pups just born and how she would bring them to see Unee when they were ready. They sat quietly in the spring sunshine, enjoying the warmth of the sun and their friendship.

Then strangers came to her village. They were different than her people, but people just the same. They brought blankets and sweet things and spoke in a strange tongue. Unee sat and listened and tried to understand. She ate their sweets and lay upon their blankets and waited for Nven to return to take her for his wife.

The red fox came to her in a dream and told her Nven was near and it made her heart glad. When she woke in the morning she tried to rise and found she was too weak. Her body felt as if it were on fire and her mouth was parched and dry. M'hati tended to her, bringing her water, cooling her with her poultices and holding her hand.

The red fox came again in a dream and told her Nven was one day away. Unee smiled in her sleep but did not awaken.

Her mother wailed and cried. Her brother brought the

clay mud from the lake and covered her with it. Still Unee's fever stayed. Then Unee's father fell ill and half the village was with fever. Open sores broke out on their bodies and they cried in their sleep. Many never woke up.

M'hati knew Unee was dying. She could not bear to lose her only daughter. She prayed to the Creator and asked for help. She sat by her daughter's side and waited for her answer.

That evening the red fox came to their home. She carried a small bundle of fur in her mouth. She padded over to where Unee lay and placed her pup on the young woman's chest. M'hati understood. The red fox was offering her the life of her pup. Unee's body would die but her soul could live on.

Unee's fever raged on and she dreamed of Nven and the forest. In her dreams she ran free and was happy. Her dreams showed her lying in the bright sun in summer and being curled up in a warm home for the winter. As the fever reached its peak, Unee smiled and became one with the pup. Then her breathing stopped. It was done.

The red fox lowered her head and walked over to Unee. She gently opened her mouth and picked up her pup by the scruff. The little one squirmed slightly and then rested in her mother's care. The mother fox brought her pup over to M'hati and lay it on the woman's lap.

M'hati gazed down and stroked the little one's soft fur. She picked it up and held it to her cheek. Her silent tears fell upon the little pup. She kissed it and lay it down beside its mother. The red fox lowered her head, picked up her pup, and returned to her den in the woods.

Nven arrived later that day, just in time to see Unee's

body being laid to rest in sacred ground.

He listened as M'hati told him of the fever and the illness and finally of the gift bestowed by the mother fox.

Nven stood silent as he stared at the burial site. His beautiful Unee was gone and he never knew her answer. He could not believe she was dead and his heart broke at the thought of never seeing her again. He walked until he could walk no more and found himself in the forest beside the lake. Unable to contain himself any longer, he began to cry. He cried for himself, for the loss he felt. He cried for Unee and he cried for her people and for all the others who died. He cried in anger and he cried in sorrow. His tears stopped for a moment and he looked down. A small stream had formed from his tears and had flowed into the lake. The lake edge shimmered and turned a beautiful real blue.

Nven chased after his tears and ran up to his waist in the lake. He shouted at the sky. "You have taken my one true love from me." Fresh tears sprang forth as Nven stood in the cool lake waters. Tiny streams of blues and greens formed all around him. He glanced towards the shore and saw the mother red fox at the edge of the thicket. She approached him cautiously and sat a safe distance away.

"Why do you stare at me sly one? Where is my Unee? What have you done with her?" Nven took a step towards the shore and then heard a soft voice in his head.

"She is safe now. She wanted me to tell you that she loved you and would have been your wife."

Nven's tears stopped for a moment. "She did? She would?" He stared at the little fox with wonder. "And would she be my wife now, with me like this? Would she be mother to my children? Tell me red one, how does love win?"

Nven noticed a movement in the thicket. Two more foxes stepped into the clearing. A mature female and a young male.

The young male walked to the edge of the water and stood in front of Nven. A voice flowed to him on the wind. "If you so desire it, this body can be yours. Death must claim your human form and then you'll be united with your Unee."

Nven sobbed and nodded. "If this be the only way, then so it shall be." He raised his arms to the sky and bellowed. "Take me from this human vessel and unite me with my one true love!"

A huge wave rose up from the lake, pulling Nven under. A few moments later, it spat him back out, his body limp and lifeless upon the shore.

No one really knows what happened after that. One thing is certain, the depth and clarity of the water in Kalamalka Lake is a beautiful sight. The ribbons of sparkling blue and green could very well be the results of true loves tears.

As for Nven and Unee, legend has it a bonded pair of foxes lived near the village for many years. They would romp and play in the sunshine, then rest upon a large rock in the clearing. Today, you might catch sight of a small red fox with a deep crimson coat, resting on the large rock on the west side of Kalamalka Lake.

THE GHOSTS OF GUISACHAN

For some people, ghost hunting is a way of life. Rachel Cardston was one of those people. She arrived at Kelowna International Airport just after 6:00 p.m. She'd flown in from Toronto to investigate certain rumours, as she called them, about recent hauntings. Although, most of her efforts resulted in debunking local stories and folklore, every now and then she found a tale without a rational explanation. It was these tales, these stories, which kept her moving from city to city.

Her actual flight time had been a little over four hours, but with layovers it had taken over seven. Flying through more than two time zones exhausted her and she looked forward to a long soak in the jacuzzi tub at the bed and breakfast. Rachel grabbed her bags from the carousel, rented a car, and inhaled the sweet smells of spring as she made her way into the city and then into the quiet neighbourhood where she had rented her room. Her host was a charming, efficient woman. She showed Rachel to her deluxe room, handed her an assortment of take out menus, and informed her breakfast was between seven and nine in the morning. Rachel thanked her and flopped onto the bed. She perused the menus, decided on Japanese, and called in her order. She grabbed her notebook and reread the information that had brought her here.

There were haunted movie theatres in Vernon, a haunted school as well. There were ghost towns and sightings all over the area. There was the Blue Lady known as Sophia who had stopped haunting the museum in Penticton once human bones were found in 1992. Over in Naramata, there was a family on horseback who disappeared into the forest and didn't leave a single hoof mark or sound as they departed. These were all interesting enough, however, the one that intrigued Rachel the most was in Kelowna with reports of a ghostly horse-driven carriage.

She flipped through her notes and read again about Lady Aberdeen and her husband, the Earl of Aberdeen. Lord and Lady Aberdeen travelled all over Canada and purchased the now haunted property from the McDougalls back in 1890. Once Lord Aberdeen was appointed Governor-General of Canada in 1893, the couple could only visit their Okanagan home during summer holidays. These rare visits set the caretaker and house staff into a flurry of preparedness.

Rachel rubbed her eyes and stared out the window. Another hour and the sun would set. Her hostess knocked at the door to let her know her food had arrived. Rachel grabbed her wallet, went downstairs, paid the delivery girl, and returned to her room.

Although it was barely 7:00 p.m. in Kelowna, it was 10:00 p.m. in Toronto and her stomach growled as she placed the bag on the desk. She ripped open the containers and dug into assorted sushi, edamame, and gomae salad. She read between bites, trying to find something new, even though she'd gone through her notes several times over the past few days.

For decades people had reported the sound of a horse-drawn carriage going down the tree-lined lane. The odd thing was there were no stories or gossip attached to this phenomenon. There was no reason for a carriage or horse being there. There were rumours of the caretaker being trigger happy, but that was it. The hauntings happened during the day and at night. She reread the story of a young girl, afraid to walk by the tree-lined driveway and feeling spooked on her way to piano lessons. Others who attended weddings and celebrations at Guisachan Park heard the clip clop of hooves, the roll of the carriage wheels. Others experienced the smell of horse droppings and cold brushing against them.

It was what wasn't reported that also piqued Rachel's interest. There were reports of sounds, smells, feelings of cold and unease, but never a visual apparition. She could find no reason for this haunting, and searching the internet proved futile. So here she was, in person, ready to find the answers.

But first, she would finish eating.

She took what was left of her meal off the desk and over to a side table that looked out over a creek and the path beside it. She could make out forms walking down the parkway. There were people of all sizes and several dogs. Not a ghost in sight.

Rachel sat back, took a sip of water, and sighed. Her obsession with ghosts had begun at an early age. Bryce Rowland, the first boy she'd ever kissed, had been there one day, and gone the next. A particularly vicious strain of pneumonia ended his young life. They'd kissed on the Thursday after her thirteenth birthday. It was a cold winter's day, but not cold enough to keep them inside. His breath was warm on her face and when his lips brushed against hers, she felt she would burst with joy. She knew in that instance, in her young and inexperienced heart, that she and Bryce were meant to be together forever.

Forever lasted two weeks. They had one glorious week of handholding, snowball fights, and cuddling in snow forts. Then one day he didn't show up at their secret spot. She went to his house, but his parents wouldn't let her in. He had a bad cold, that's all, nothing to worry about. The following Monday there was an announcement at assembly in the gym. Bryce had died. Classmates were invited to sign a card for his parents. That was it. Nothing more was said, nothing more was done. There was no funeral, no celebration of life. Bryce's mother took to her bed and never fully recovered. Rachel overhead her parents talk about how devastating losing a child would be, then they both came into her room and hugged her tight. She wanted to scream and tell them he wasn't a child. He was her boyfriend and they had kissed and were going to be together forever. Instead, she let them hug her and when they left, she cried herself to sleep. There was no place to visit to say goodbye. Bryce was cremated and his remains were shipped off to a family plot somewhere in southern Ontario. His parents moved away shortly thereafter, and Rachel was left with an aching heart and a need to reconcile her loss. She tried to contact Bryce on an old Ouija board she'd found in the basement, but he never came through. She would wake from a dream once in a while and hear him calling her. In her dreams she could feel his warm breath on her face, his lips brush against hers, and then he was gone, and she would find herself alone in the dark.

Here she was, sixteen years later, eating take-out Japanese food at a bed and breakfast and still searching for answers. Only now she was getting paid to find them. She'd graduated from high school and gone to university to study psychology. That led to parapsychology, and eventually she was accepted to the research team at the Centre for the Study of Anomalous Psychological Processes at the University of Northampton. Even that did not give her the answers she desperately needed, so she joined a private paranormal investigative firm in Toronto who did research for various TV and movie projects. Now she was chasing ghosts in the Okanagan in British Columbia. Much to her disappointment the majority of ghost sightings she investigated brought her no closer to answers. Even though some cases were unexplained, and made great fodder for TV and movie fans, she had not found absolute proof that ghosts or spirits existed.

Rachel sighed as she gathered up the food containers and placed them in the garbage. She needed that soak now that her tummy was full, and she was going to enjoy every second of it. Her bathroom had an impressive assortment of bath salts and bubble bath lining the counter by the jacuzzi tub. She sniffed a few and settled on the lavender. An aromatic bouquet of bubbles formed as she turned on the jets, undressed, and stepped into the tub. She sighed again, letting herself sink into the encompassing warmth. After a short time, she turned off the jets, closed her eyes, and listened to the quiet.

She sensed him before she saw him. She felt the warmth of his breath on her cheek and waited in anticipation for the kiss that was sure to come. She shivered and waited. Then she reached up her hand to touch his face and connected with air. Another shiver shook her as she opened her eyes. It was pitch black and the water was cold. She jumped out of the tub, grabbed a towel, and made her way to the bed. The clock on the nightstand read 10:00 p.m. She'd been in the tub for almost two hours. No wonder she was cold. She dried herself and changed into an old T-shirt. She wondered for a moment if she'd be able to sleep so soon after her little water nap. Moments after snuggling down into the bed, she drifted into a dreamless slumber.

The sun shoved its way through a crack in the curtain and focused a beam of light on Rachel's nose. She opened her eyes and stretched. The thought of ghost hunting in broad daylight was a bit against the norm, however, Rachel felt certain today was the day she'd find a real, honest to goodness ghost. She was delighted to discover a full breakfast waiting for her in the dining room and she ate it with gusto. Ghost hunting always made her hungry. She asked the other bed and breakfast guests and her host if they'd heard stories about the ghosts at Guisachan. No one had. Undaunted, Rachel headed off in her rental car. Trees were budding, flowers poking out of once dormant beds, and the smell of freshly mown grass enveloped her.

She pulled into the parking lot and looked at a map to familiarize herself with the area. Most of the reports had come from the allée, a driveway lined with Eastern white cedars that were planted by Lady Aberdeen around 1892. It was here where the horse and carriage was heard over the past century or so. Rachel headed towards the trees. A breeze played with her hair as she walked the old road and admired the tall cedars with their bright green foliage. She stopped for a moment and waited. No naying of horses, no smell of manure, no cool breeze, no rolling buggy wheels.

She closed her eyes, eased her head back, and drew in a deep breath. A memory seeped from the depths of her being and then disappeared as she exhaled. She felt the shadow of the leaves on her face as the sun warmed the land around her. She stayed in that position for a moment, eyes closed, head back, arms relaxed at her side. Perhaps if she looked around a bit more, she'd discover something.

She opened her eyes and watched the trees shimmering in the sunlight. Maybe she was looking in the wrong spot. She walked off the road and through the trees into a field.

Something felt off, not ghostly, just off. The ground

beneath her was slightly uneven and some of the plants and tufts of brush she navigated around were larger than expected. There was something missing as well, but she couldn't put her finger on it. She turned to look behind her and saw a man her age step through the trees. When he saw her, his face broke into a wide smile and he ran towards her.

"I can't believe I found you here!" He was dressed in old work clothes and an old-fashioned farmers hat. His smile lit up his tanned face.

"Just looking for ghosts," Rachel replied, and let out a small laugh realizing how odd that must sound.

"I can assure you I am not a ghost." He took off his hat, revealing a shock of unruly brown hair. "You shouldn't be here. This is private property. I've been looking everywhere for you. You could have been mistaken as a trespasser and shot. Then you'd be a ghost."

Rachel shook her head. "But I thought … isn't this a public park?"

The man chuckled and shook his head. "Stop playing around now. Come on, let me get you home."

Rachel was certain, from looking at her map, that this was also part of the land belonging to Guisachan House. Not that it mattered what the map said at this point, she was clearly not where she was supposed to be. No wonder she didn't hear any ghostly hoof beats.

"Coming?" the young man interrupted her thoughts and extended his hand.

"Yes, of course." Rachel reached for his hand. In an

instant, she felt a familiarity, a memory. "Do I know you?" she asked as they made their way towards the trees. Part of her knew she was behaving rather recklessly. After all, who in their right mind would take a stranger's hand and run through a field with them. Another part didn't care. What had come over her? Who was this man?

He stopped at the edge of the road and let her go. "Do you know me? What nonsense is that now?" He stepped forward and cupped her head in his rough hands. She felt his breathe on her face and she inhaled sharply as his lips brushed hers.

She pulled back and stared. "Bryce?" It couldn't be him. He was dead, long dead, yet this kiss was familiar, comforting.

He laughed. "Well, I should hope so. There better not be any other men wandering around kissing my wife. Now come on before they find us here and start shooting."

He led her towards a waiting buggy. The horses whinnied and pawed at the ground. "Wife? What? But?" Rachel stammered. Could this be the first visual sighting of a human Guisachan ghost? Was Bryce a ghost?

He helped her onto the seat of the buggy and kissed her once more. "You know, I thought I'd lost you. They're getting the place ready for Lord and Lady Aberdeen's return next month and I heard a rumour in town last night that the groundskeeper had gone a little crazy and shot a trespasser out here."

"Shooting trespassers? What are you talking about?" She looked around as he grabbed the reins and urged the horses forward. She couldn't see the parking lot but she knew they were headed in the wrong direction. "My car … it's back there."

"There's nothing back there but a crazed estate guard who'll shoot at anything that moves."

The buggy continued down the driveway and turned right on a dirt road. "They told me being with child would change you, but I didn't count on you wandering off and forgetting me." Bryce stopped the buggy, turned, and held Rachel in his arms. "Please don't ever do that again."

Rachel was stunned. She reached down and felt the swell of her belly and the roughness of her dress. Where were her jeans? Bryce leaned in and kissed her again.

A sense of calm washed over her as she closed her eyes and breathed in the fresh spring air. She opened her eyes and smiled up at a man she knew she loved. "Take me home."

NAJ AND THE TRICKSTER

I t was a perfect spring day. The kind of day Naj loved as the people in his village were busy with other things, which made it easy to sneak up on them. Naj stealthily made his way to a group of children playing a game of stones. He kept close to the tipis and crawled on the ground around the kekuli huts. He was right behind them and waited for the right moment.

"ARRRHWHAARR!" he shouted. The children dropped their stones, screamed and ran for their mothers. The women glared at Naj and shooed him away. Grandfather watched the scene unfold as he sat in front of his kekuli hut, methodically stirring ingredients in a pot. He called for Naj to join him.

"Why should I?" Naj said as he walked towards the old

man and then sat beside him.

"Because you are young and foolish and you have a great gift," replied Grandfather. "You are as quiet as an eagle soaring high in the sky and have the swiftness of a fox. You could be a great hunter one day, yet instead of learning this skill, you stay with the women, children, and elders."

"The men and older boys are gone for days," said Naj. "They walk for miles looking for signs and they sleep on the ground without blankets. Father told me they sit quietly for hours and wait for the animals they hunt. I can't sit that long." Naj dipped a finger in the medicine pot, then put his finger to his nose and sniffed. He made a nasty face and wiped his finger in the dirt.

"Then be the runner," the old man offered as he added a pinch of dried bark into the pot. "Be the one who brings news from our hunters to their families. Be the one who runs quietly and effortlessly home with tales of a successful hunt. Be the bringer of information."

"There's no fun in that." Naj shook his head and leapt to his feet, stirring dust up around him.

The old man placed his hand over the pot and coughed softly. "The hunters are returning tonight, Naj. Speak to them, find out where you fit."

Naj looked down at the old man. "They'll have to catch me first," he shouted as he ran behind Grandfather's hut.

Grandfather shook his head and slowly got to his feet. He hoped the potion he was making would cure Naj of his mischievous ways. He went inside to search for the last few ingredients he needed.

Trickster watched from the hillside. He crept into the village and sat beside the bubbling pot. Smiling, he plucked a burr and a handful of fur from his underbelly, stirred them into the pot with his long claw, then slipped back into the hills.

Grandfather emerged from his hut and added the last few ingredients. He would paint Naj with the potion right before the feast. If it worked, Naj would stop his mischief making and become a great hunter. Grandfather said a prayer over the pot and waited.

Just then a great outcry was heard beyond the village. Naj raced to his grandfather, kicking up dust as he ran. He was out of breath and sweating. "Oh Grandfather, you must hide me," he cried.

"What have you done now?" asked Grandfather for what he hoped would be the last time.

"You should have seen those brave warriors when I jumped out from behind a rock. They dropped the deer and pheasants and reached for their spears. Hide me!"

Grandfather grabbed the pot off the fire and led Naj inside. "Sit," he said, pointing to a spot on the floor. Naj did as he was told. Grandfather picked up a thick feather and dipped it into the pot. "This will help hide you," he said as he drew diamond shapes on Naj's bare chest, arms and legs. He carefully drew black lines around the boy's eyes.

"That tickles." Naj swatted at the feather.

"Hush boy," said Grandfather as he continued to paint. After a few more strokes he stepped back to look at his work.

"That should do. Now, just one more diamond."

"No." Naj stood and bolted outside. Grandfather went after him, but Naj was nowhere to be seen.

That night the entire tribe gathered for the feast. Nuts and roots were roasted in the fire and laid out with the berries and the freshly cooked deer and pheasant. Children fell asleep on their mothers' laps as the men retold the tale of the hunt. Then they told of Naj and how he had snuck up on them just before they entered the village. There was praise for his stealth and talk of punishment for his foolishness. It was decided Naj would go on a private hunting trip with two of their best hunters in the morning. He would not be allowed back until he had caught a rabbit with his own hands. The men laughed and stories were told of their first hunts, the first time they'd caught a rabbit.

Families disbanded and went to their homes, bellies full and heads swimming with stories of the hunt. The fires died down and Naj was nowhere to be seen. Grandfather scanned the hills, sighed, and retired to his comfortable bed for the night.

High above the village in the rolling hills, Naj lay curled in an indent in the sand and rock. His eyes closed as the last embers of his small fire died out. He fell into a deep and dreamless sleep.

Naj awoke to the feel of the sun warming his skin. Eyes still closed, he moved his head from side to side, stretched his torso, and tried to stretch his arms. They didn't move. Naj's eyes flew open. His arms were gone. He looked down and saw one long leg covered in the diamonds his grandfather had painted on him. Instead of a foot, there was a nub at the end.

Naj held back his tears as fear coursed through his body. He mentally examined this new body of his and realized he could move by contracting the muscles in his belly and what used to be his legs. He zig-zagged his way down the hillside to grandfather's hut, but grandfather wasn't there. He slithered inside and waited in a corner. He could hear the men calling his name from different parts of the valley.

"I'm here!" he cried out, but all that came out of his mouth was a raspy hissing sound.

"They can't hear you," said Trickster. He appeared in front of Naj and sniffed at Naj's tail. "Ah, no rattles yet. You'll get them soon enough. You'll shed your skin two or three times over the next year and each time you'll get another rattle. Then, once you have a big enough rattle, you won't be able to sneak up on people. But they might sneak up on you and try to eat you for dinner."

Trickster laughed at the thought of Naj being frightened as much as he had frightened others.

"A year," Naj hissed. "Why did you do this to me?"

Trickster sat on his haunches and smiled. "Because I can," he replied. "You were ruining my fun. I can't have that. I am the trickster, I am the mischief maker, not you. Know your place boy."

Trickster turned to go as Grandfather entered. The pair stared at each other warily. Wordlessly the pair sat across from each other.

Naj let out a soft hiss. Grandfather looked closely at the snake, then at Trickster.

"I've taken care of our problem," said Trickster as he pointed to Naj. "I'm sure once the boy has spent twelve or fourteen moons as a snake, he'll stop being such a mischief maker."

"Naj?" Grandfather approached the snake and looked into its eyes. "Oh, Naj, I warned you. Now look at yourself."

Naj curled into a circle and hid his head under his tail. Grandfather picked up Naj and hugged him.

"Careful," said Trickster as he left the hut. "He may be your grandson, but he's still a rattlesnake."

Grandfather placed Naj carefully in a pouch and took him high into the hills. He found a sunny spot, crouched down, and let Naj out of the pouch. The snake slithered away and hid behind some sun-warmed rocks. He poked his head out as Grandfather spoke.

"If you are patient, it shouldn't take long for you to catch something for dinner. And you'll have to be still, because in a few months, you'll have a rattle and they will hear you." Grandfather sighed, bent over to pat the snake, then changed his mind. "I'll tell the others," he said. "I'll come back now and then to check on you."

Naj tried to speak but he couldn't quite remember what he wanted to say. A small mouse skittered past his grandfather's foot. Naj lurched forward, mouth open, and clamped down on the hapless creature. Within a few seconds the struggling stopped and Naj swallowed it whole. Satisfied, he went back behind the rocks to sun himself.

T his is one of those tales that sounds like a far-fetched story. I'll tell you right now, this story is the truth, or at least as much truth as one can find nowadays.

Here in the Okanagan we have an abundance of a strange bird. This bird is known as the quail. They are considered to be a game bird and there are approximately thirty-one species. They are known by many names including California Quail, San Quentin Quail, and Top Knot Quail.

This is a tale about these seemingly harmless birds and the games they play on the innocent inhabitants of the Okanagan Valley.

One of these inhabitants was known as Mary. At least

that's what she said it was. She could have given me an alias to protect herself, after all, you never know who may read this.

One summer she came for a visit from the Yukon and fell in love with the Okanagan Valley. By the following spring she had moved to Penticton. She said she loved it here, loved the peace and quiet, especially the warmth.

Her peace of mind was shattered a few hours after she unpacked her last box. She became a player in one of the quails' unruly little games. I believe the culprits of the day were the San Quentin Quail, the hardened descendants of the criminal birds from California.

For Mary, it started out to be the perfect day. The Okanagan sun was shining, the fruit stands were open, and the farmers market carried an abundance of fresh fruits, veggies, and crafts. It was a perfect Saturday afternoon. Her shopping complete, she decided to explore her new town.

Mary was an adventurous sort. I say *was*, because since this experience, she doesn't venture very far. On that day, however, she was feeling adventurous and decided to drive around and view some of the famed gardens she'd heard so much about. It was a decision she would regret forever.

She should have known the back alleys weren't safe. Someone should have warned her. She was so naive then, so unaware of the marauding hordes that roamed the alleys and darkened the scrub of the Okanagan.

On that fateful day, Mary turned left down an alley. A beautiful garden had caught her eye and she wanted a better look. Such an innocent reason, such an innocent woman.

She was admiring the pinks and purples of the garden when they appeared. They'd camouflaged themselves in the brush beside the roadway and as soon as Mary moved past the garden the entire gang rushed her car. They came at her like a squad of deranged Lilliputians. To this day she swears she can still hear their cries.

"We're crazy, we're crazy, we're crazy!"

They came at her from the left and the right. They landed on the hood of her car. She slammed on the brakes, fearful she would crush one of these tiny beings. When the car stopped, they slowed down.

She looked behind her to see if there was a way she could back out of this sea of crazy quail, but they were behind her, too. There she was, trapped by her inability to run over small, feathered creatures. They stopped, stared at her, and then walked in front of the car. She was snared in a net of quail. The one she assumed to be the leader walked quickly ahead, the little knot on his head bobbing bizarrely in the mid-day sun. More males and females joined in, and finally the little ones took their place in the macabre parade.

Mary couldn't understand how it had come to this. Where were they taking her? Somehow the birds knew her prime directive was to do no harm and they were using it against her.

Down the alley they went. Mary was frantic with worry. Would she run one over? Would they attack her? She shuddered as she recalled the Hitchcock movie, *The Birds*. She wished she had left the top up on her convertible. A young female was perched on her hood. It stared at her with black, beady eyes.

Mary told me she was on the verge of tears when all of a sudden there rose the maniacal battle cry. "We're crazy! We're crazy! We're crazy!"

As quickly as they had descended upon her, they were gone. She was left alone and trembling in the bright sunlight of an eerily strange day.

Mary packed up and moved that very day. She called me from the Yukon when she arrived. She said the weather wasn't as nice, but the animals kept their distance.

Acknowledgements

Special thanks go out to LeEtta LaFontaine for doing such a great job of interpreting my stories with her art work.

I also want to thank all my clients, students, and readers who have believed in me throughout this journey. From the bottom of my heart, I thank you. Let's keep going!

About the Author

Darcy Nybo developed a love for writing in grade two. She put together her first book by cutting out pictures, pasting them into a notebook, then adding her own words.

You could say it was her first attempt at being a published author.

A few months later she wrote a short story about a young boy who earned money to buy a new wagon by selling turnips.

In retrospect, at the age of seven, she already had the makings of an author and entrepreneur.

Darcy' believes her writing has improved somewhat since then. She is a multiple award-winning short story author, a freelance writer and editor for several magazines, a web writer with a focus on SEO, a team publisher, a writing coach, and a marketing maven. When she isn't writing, editing or coaching, you'll find her teaching creative and business writing.

Darcy's entrepreneurial spirit is strong. In the mid 1990s she created a successful local newspaper which she sold in the early 2000s. In 2004 she created Always Write (alwayswrite. ca) a freelance writing and SEO company. A few years later she started Artistic Warrior (artisticwarrior.com) a hybrid/team publishing company where she coaches authors, edits, and does layout for her clients. She then assists them in getting their books into the hands of readers.

She's also written several children's books, including an Okanagan activity book (*Great Grape Adventure*) and two picture books for primary school readers, (*Emma Jean Finds a Friend* and *Bark, Swat, Crunch!*). They are all available on Amazon.

She is currently putting together a second book of short stories and working on her second novel while she discovers if she really does have a talent for painting.

About the Illustrator

LeEtta LaFontaine is an accomplished artist who has experienced success in many mediums. Drawing is LeEtta's passion, especially with charcoal on canvas. An image rendered in pencil or charcoal has a timeless quality and soon becomes a family heirloom.

LeEtta has co-authored books of sketches and photography. She has exhibited her work in shows throughout BC as well as in the PNE show home.

You can find her on Facebook at facebook.com/leetta. artist

www.ingramcontent.com/pod-product-compliance
Lightning Source LLC
Chambersburg PA
CBHW071236170626
46809CB00008BA/3085